Goldie and the Toys

~ & ~

The Toys go to the Seaside

Published in 2004 by Mercury Books London
20 Bloomsbury Street, London WC1B 3JH

© text copyright Enid Blyton Limited
© copyright original illustrations, Hodder and Stoughton Limited
© new illustrations 2004 Mercury Books London

Designed and produced for Mercury Books
by Open Door Limited, Langham, Rutland

Title: Goldie and the Toys & The Toys go to the Seaside
ISBN: 1 904668 30 5

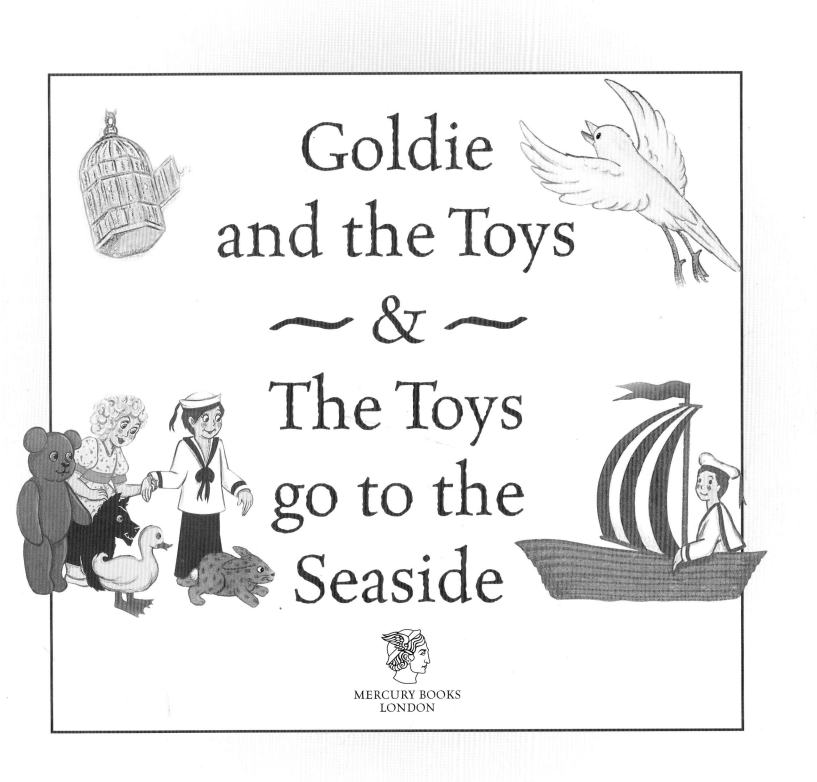

Goldie
and the Toys
~ & ~
The Toys
go to the
Seaside

MERCURY BOOKS
LONDON

Goldie and the Toys

Once there was a canary in a cage. The bird was as yellow as gold, so he was called Goldie. He belonged to Eric and Hilda, and they were very fond of him; they cleaned out his cage every day and gave him fresh food and water.

Now every night he used to watch the toys come alive and play with one another. He would peep out of his cage with his bright black eyes and long to get out and play with the dolls and animals. They had such good times.

"Do open my cage door and let me out!" he would beg each night. "I want to dance with the curly-haired doll! I want to ride in that big train! I want to wind up the musical box and hear it sing. Oh, do let me out, toys!"

But they wouldn't, for they knew that he might escape out of the nursery, and then Eric

and Hilda would be very sad.
So they shook their heads and
went on playing by themselves.

But one night, after Christmas,
there was a new toy in the
nursery. This was
a green duck, and it liked the
look of the yellow canary very
much. So when the little bird
began to call out to the toys
to let it out of its cage,
the duck spoke up.

"Why don't we let the canary out to have a bit of fun with us? After all, the poor thing is stuck in its cage all day long and never gets a chance to play a game. I'd like to be friends with it. I'm a bird, too, and I should like a good long chat with another bird."

"Yes, yes!" cried the canary eagerly. "Let me out, duck! I am so lonely up here! I should love a chat with a beautiful bird like you!"

"The windows and the door are shut," said the big doll. "I don't see that it will do any harm. The canary couldn't escape out of the room if it wanted to!"

"I don't want to escape!" cried the canary. "I just want to have a game. I will go back to my cage when everything is over."

"Very well," said the biggest doll. "You shall come out and join us this evening – but remember, if you don't behave properly, we'll never let you out again!"

The canary promised to be good, and the toy clown threw a rope up to the cage, and then climbed right up to it. He opened the door and out flew Goldie, simply delighted to stretch his wings and have a fly round.

You should have seen how Goldie enjoyed himself. The toys set the musical box going and when the tune was tinkled out the canary took hold of the curly-haired doll with his wing and off they danced together over the nursery floor.

The canary really danced very well indeed, for he was so light on his feet.

After they had had a good dance, the clockwork train offered to take the toys for a ride. Of course, the canary wanted to drive, and, my goodness me, he drove so fast that the train couldn't see where it was going,

and bumped
into a chair leg.
Out fell all the toys in
a heap, and they were not
very pleased with the canary.

13

He didn't get bumped at all because as soon as he saw the engine was going to run into the chair leg he simply spread his wings and flew safely into the air!

Then the toys played hide-and-seek, and the canary liked that very much because he could fly up to the top of the curtains, or on to the clock, and no toys thought of looking there for him, so he was the only one that was never caught. He did enjoy himself.

At last cockcrow came, when all the toys had to go back to the toy-cupboard and sleep.

"It's time to go back to
your cage, Goldie,"
said the big doll;
"You've had a lovely
time, haven't you?
Just fly back to your
cage now, there's a good bird, and let the
clockwork clown shut your door."

"Not I!" said Goldie cheekily. "I'm not going
back to my cage for hours and HOURS and
HOURS. No, I'm going to stay in the nursery
and fly about as long as I like!"

"But you promised!" cried the toys.

"I don't care!" said the naughty canary.

"How dreadful to break a promise!" said
the green duck, who was feeling hurt because
the canary had hardly spoken a word to him.
"I wonder you're not ashamed of yourself.
Go back to your cage at once."

But the canary simply wouldn't. He just flew away as soon as any toy came near him. It was most annoying.

"We shall have to do something!" said the big doll in despair. "If we leave him loose like this he will fly out of the door in the morning when the housemaid opens it, and then the cat will get him! What can we do?"

They all whispered together, and then at last the clockwork clown had an idea.

"Let's spread the table in the dolls' house, and say we're going to have supper there," he said. "The canary will want to join us, of course – and we'll get him in. Then we'll all go out and slam the door. He will have to stay in the dolls' house till morning then."

"Splendid idea!" cried all the toys. They ran to the dolls' house, and began to lay the cloth. They set out the tiny cups, saucers and plates, and then the big doll fetched some sweets from the toy sweet-shop.

"What are you doing?" cried the canary from his perch on a candlestick.

"We're going to have supper," said the clockwork clown.

"Well, I'm coming, too," said the canary.

Down he flew and hopped in at the front door of the dolls' house. The curly-haired doll saw that all the windows were tightly shut, and the clockwork clown stuffed up the chimney with paper so that Goldie couldn't escape that way.

The canary sat down on a chair, and the big doll gave him a sweet on his plate. He put it into his beak, and didn't notice that one by one all the toys were creeping out of the house. At last he was quite alone.

Slam! The canary jumped up in fright. The door of the dolls' house was tight shut. He was caught.

"Let me out, let me out!" he yelled.

"No," said the toys. "You just stay here!"

"Let me go back to my cage," said the canary.

"No," said the big doll at once. "As soon as we open the door you would fly away again!"

"I promise I would go back to my cage," said Goldie, pecking the front door with his beak.

"We don't trust you," said the clown. "You broke your promise before, so we are sure you would break it again." Then the toys went to the toy cupboard and fell asleep.

The canary hopped on the table of the dolls' house and went to sleep too.

In the morning Eric and Hilda came into the nursery – and the first thing they saw was the open door of the canary's cage. How upset they were!

"Goldie's gone, Goldie's gone!" they cried, "Oh, where can he be?"

Goldie heard his name and he hopped about excitedly in the dolls' house, trilling loudly.

"Listen!" said Eric, astonished. "Can you hear Goldie trilling? Where is he?"

"It sounds as if he were in the dolls' house!" said Hilda, astonished. They knelt down and peeped through the window – and there they saw Goldie, hopping about inside the little house.

"There he is!" said Eric. "But however did he get there? What a funny thing! He can't have got in there and shut the door himself!"

The children opened the door and Eric slipped in his hand and took hold of Goldie very gently – and in two seconds the little canary was safely in his cage once more, singing very loudly indeed.

"I'm sure our big doll is smiling," said Hilda suddenly. "I wonder why?"

"Perhaps she could tell us how Goldie got into the dolls' house!" said Eric.

She certainly could, couldn't she? You may be quite sure that the toys never let Goldie out of his cage again. He really was much too naughty to be trusted!

The Toys go to the Seaside

Once upon a time the goblin Peeko put his head in at the nursery and cried. "Who wants a day at the seaside?"

The toys sat up with a jerk. They were all alone in the nursery, for Tom and Beryl, whose toys they were, had gone away to stay at their Granny's. The toys were

really feeling rather dull.
A day at the seaside
sounded simply gorgeous!

"How do we go?" asked the pink rabbit.

"By bus," said the goblin grinning. "My bus.
I bought it yesterday. Penny each all the way there."

"Ooooh!" said the sailor doll, longingly. "I
would like to see the sea. I've never been there
– and it's dreadful to be a sailor doll and not
to know what the sea is like, really it is!"

"Come on, then," said Peeko.

"Climb out of the window, all of you.

There's plenty of room in the bus."

So the pink rabbit, the sailor doll, the yellow duck, the walking doll, the black dog, and the blue teddy bear all climbed out of the window and got into the goblin's bus, which was standing on the path outside.

The goblin took the wheel. The bus gave a roar and a jolt that sent the pink rabbit nearly through the roof – and it was off!

It was a fine journey to the sea. The goblin knew all the shortest cuts. It wasn't long before the sailor doll gave a yell and cried, "The sea! The sea!"

"Pooh!" said the goblin. "That's just a duck-pond."

"But aren't those gulls sailing on it?" asked the doll.

"No, ducks!" said Peeko.

"Quack, quack!" said the yellow toy duck, and laughed loudly at the sailor doll. After that the doll didn't say anything at all, not even when they came to the real sea and saw it glittering and shining in the sun. He was afraid it might be a duck-pond too – or an extra big puddle!

They all tumbled out of the bus
and ran on to the beach.
"I'm off for a swim!"
said the yellow duck.

"I'd like a sail in a boat!"
said the sailor doll. "Oh! There's
a nice little boat over there, just my size."
It belonged to a little boy. He had gone home
to dinner and had forgotten to take his boat
with him. The sailor doll ran to it, pushed it
out on to the sea, jumped aboard and was
soon enjoying himself!

The pink rabbit thought he would like to make himself a burrow in the sand. It was always difficult to dig a burrow in the nursery. Now he really would be able to dig, and showered sand all over the blue teddy bear.

"Hi, hi, pink rabbit, what are you doing?" cried the bear. But the pink rabbit was already deep in the sandy tunnel, enjoying himself thoroughly, and didn't hear the bear's shout.

"I shall have a nap," said the blue teddy bear. "Don't disturb me, anybody."

He lay down on the soft yellow sand and shut his eyes. Soon a deep growly snore was heard.

The black dog giggled and looked at the walking-doll. "Shall we bury him in sand?" he wuffed. "He would be so surprised when he woke up and found himself a sandy bear."

"Yes, let's" said the doll. So they began to bury the sleeping teddy bear in the sand. They piled it over his legs, they piled it over his fat little tummy, they piled it over his arms.

They didn't put any on his head, so all that could be seen of the bear was just his blunt blue snout sticking up. He did look funny.

"I'm off for a walk," said the walking-doll. "This beach is a good place to stretch my legs. I never can walk very far in the nursery – only round and round and round."

She set off over the beach,
her long legs twinkling
in and out. The black dog
was alone. What
should he do?

"The sailor doll is sailing.
The yellow duck is swimming.
The pink rabbit is burrowing. The teddy bear is
sleeping. The walking-doll is walking. I think I
will go and sniff round for a big fat bone,"

said the black dog. So off he went.

Now when Peeko the goblin came
on the beach two or three hours
later, to tell the toys that it was time
to go home, do you think he could see
a single one? No! There didn't seem to be
anyone in sight at all! Peeko was annoyed.

"Just like them to disappear when it's time
to go home," he said crossly.
"Well, I suppose I must just wait for them,
that's all. I'll sit down.

Peeko looked for a nice place to sit. He saw a soft-looking humpy bit of sand. It was really the teddy bear's tummy, buried in the sand, but he didn't know that. He walked over to the humpy bit and sat down in the middle of it.

The blue bear woke up with a jump.

"Oooourrrrrrr," he growled, and sat up suddenly. The goblin fell over in fright. The bear snapped at him and growled again. Then saw it was Peeko.

"What do you mean by sitting down in the middle of me like that?" he said crossly.

"How should I know it was the middle of you when you were all buried in sand?" said Peeko.

"I wasn't," said the bear, in surprise, for he had no idea he had been buried.

"You were," said Peeko.

"I wasn't," said the bear.

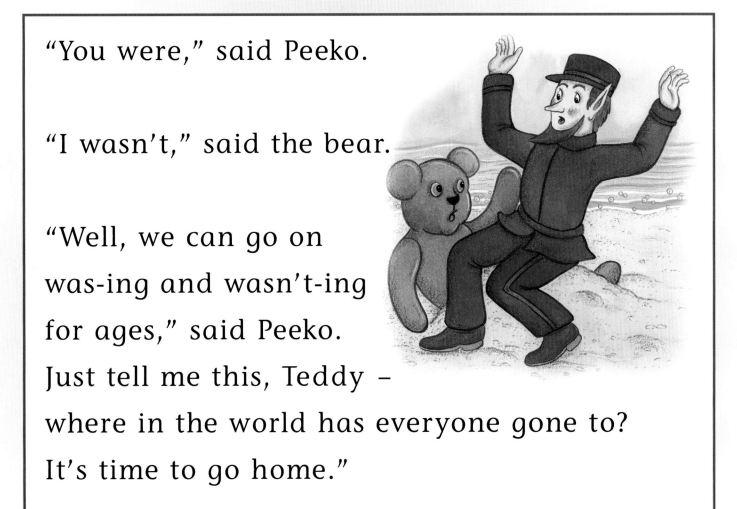

"Well, we can go on was-ing and wasn't-ing for ages," said Peeko. Just tell me this, Teddy – where in the world has everyone gone to? It's time to go home."

"Is it really?" said the bear, astonished. "Dear me, it seems as if we've only just come!"

"I don't see why you wanted to come at all if all you do is snore," said Peeko. "Waste of a penny, I call it!"

"Well, if you think that, I won't give you my penny," said the teddy, at once.

"Don't be silly," said the goblin. "Look here, bear, if we don't start soon it will be too late. What am I to do? I'd better go without you."

"Oh no, don't do that," said the bear in alarm. "I'll soon get the others back.

We have a special whistle that we use when it's time to go home." He pursed up his teddy bear mouth and whistled. It was a shrill, loud whistle, and every one of the toys heard it. You should have seen them rushing back to the beach!

The sailor doll sailed his ship proudly to shore, jumped out, and pulled the ship onto the sand. He really did feel a sailor now!

The yellow duck came quacking and swimming in, bobbing up and down in delight. She waddled up the beach, and shook her feathers, sending a shower of drops all over Peeko, who was most annoyed.

The walking-doll tore back across the beach. The black dog came running up carrying an enormous bone in his mouth, very old and smelly. The toys looked at it in disgust.

"Where's the pink rabbit?" asked Peeko. "He would be last!" The toys giggled. Peeko was standing at the entrance of the pink rabbit's burrow, but he didn't know he was! The toys knew what would happen – and it did!

The pink rabbit had heard the bear's whistling. He was coming back along his burrow. He suddenly shot out, all legs and sand – and Peeko felt his legs bumped hard, and he sat down very suddenly! The pink rabbit had come out in a great hurry, just between the goblin's legs. The toys laughed till they cried. Peeko was quite angry. "First I sit on a hump that isn't a hump and get a dreadful fright!" he said. "And then I get bowled over by a silly rabbit who comes out of the sand. Get into the bus all of you, before I say I won't take you home."

They all got into the bus. Most of them were tired and sleepy now, all except the teddy bear, who was very lively indeed – but then, he had been asleep all the time!

They climbed in at the nursery window. They each gave Peeko a penny, and he drove his bus away quietly, and parked it under the lilac bush. The toys crept into the cupboard and sat as still as could be.

And when Tom and Beryl came back the next day from their Granny's they were surprised to see how well and brown their toys all looked.

"Just as if they had been to the sea!" said Tom.

"Don't be silly, Tom!" said Beryl. But he wasn't silly! They had been to the sea!

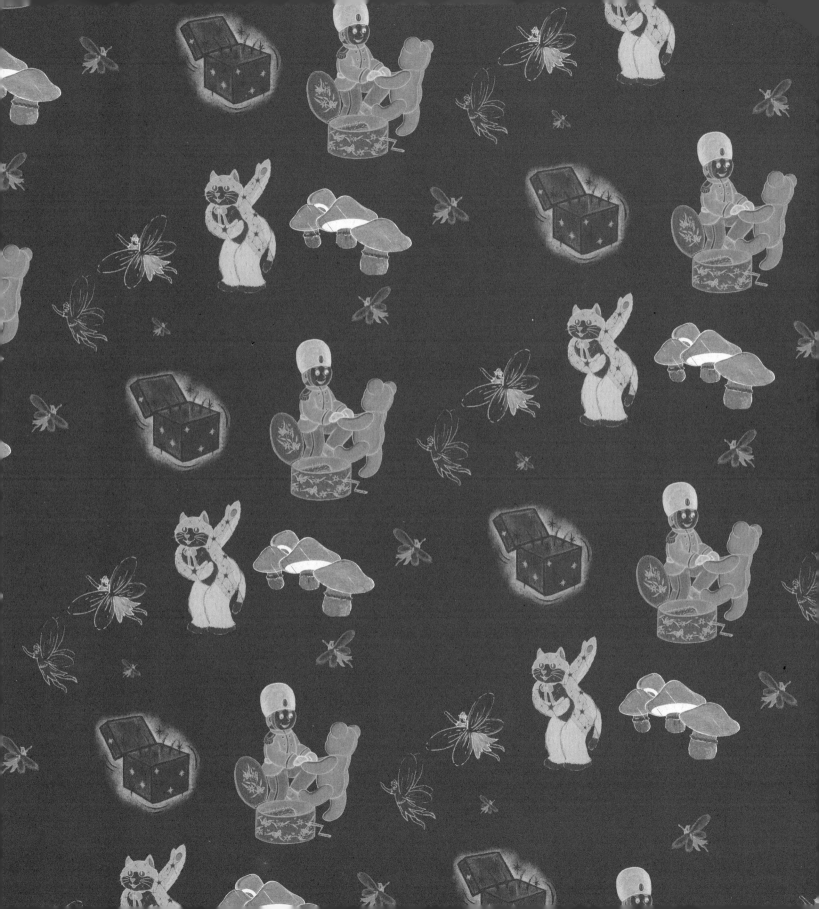